木	Tree	*mù* *(moo)*
	休	Rest	*xiū* *(seeyou)*
	林	Forest	*lín* *(lin)*
	淋	Pond	*lín* *(lin)*
	雨	Rain	*yǔ* *(you*, pronounced with rounded lips)

Pronunciation of words in parentheses
are approximations of Mandarin Chinese.

For W. L. and M. H.—Thank you for always believing in me.

AUTHOR'S NOTE

The Chinese language uses pictures—instead of letters—for words. The pronunciation guide used here is from the Mandarin dialect, which is the national language of China, but there are more than eight hundred different Chinese dialects and subdialects. Written Chinese is shared by more than one billion people, and although many of them cannot understand one another's speech, they can all read the same language.

Henry Holt and Company, LLC, *Publishers since 1866*
115 West 18th Street, New York, New York 10011

Henry Holt is a registered trademark of Henry Holt and Company, LLC

Copyright © 1995 by Huy Voun Lee
All rights reserved.
Published in Canada by Fitzhenry & Whiteside Ltd., 195 Allstate Parkway, Markham, Ontario L3R 4T8.

Library of Congress Cataloging-in-Publication Data
Lee, Huy Voun.
In the snow / by Huy Voun Lee.
Summary: A mother and son practice writing Chinese characters in the snow. Introduces the characters for ten simple words.
[1. Snow—Fiction. 2. Mothers and sons—Fiction. 3. Chinese Americans—Fiction. 4. Chinese language—Vocabulary.] I. Title.
PZ7.L51248In 1995 [E]—dc20 94-48807

ISBN 0-8050-3172-3 (hardcover)
1 3 5 7 9 10 8 6 4 2
ISBN 0-8050-6579-2 (paperback)
1 3 5 7 9 10 8 6 4 2

First published in hardcover in 1995 by Henry Holt and Company
First Owlet paperback edition—2000
The artist used cut-paper collage to create the illustrations for this book.
Printed in the United States of America on acid-free paper. ∞

下雪天
IN THE SNOW

Written and illustrated by

Huy Voun Lee

Henry Holt and Company / New York

It is a wonderful day for a walk in the forest. It is winter, the first snow has fallen, and the ground is a canvas of white.

Today Xiao Ming's mother is helping him learn new Chinese characters. Writing Chinese is fun for Xiao Ming because he thinks it is just like drawing pictures.

木 With a stick from a fallen branch, Xiao Ming's mother draws in the snow. "This is the character for *tree,*" she says.

"It looks just like a tree. I can see its trunk, branches, and roots," exclaims Xiao Ming.

"That's right," answers his mother. "The symbol for *tree* also means *wood*."

林 "What character does it make when we put two *trees* together?"
"*Forest,* because many trees together make a forest."

淋 "Now, if I add three strokes next to the character for *forest,* can you guess what word it makes?" his mother asks.

"Let's see, three strokes always means *water.* Water in the forest . . . *pond,* right?" answers Xiao Ming.

"Right, Xiao Ming!"

休 "I know another word that uses the character for *tree*," says Xiao Ming as he draws in the snow. "When I draw a hooked line next to *tree*, it means *rest*. See, I imagine a person leaning against a tree."

雨 "You have a great imagination, Xiao Ming," says his mother. "Will it help you to remember the character for *rain*?"

"That's a hard one. . . ."

"Watch carefully." His mother draws in the snow as she explains. "Not all characters look exactly like pictures. But if you use your imagination again, you'll see drops of water falling from a cloud."

雪 Xiao Ming tosses a snowball to his mother. "How do I write *snow*?" he asks.
"Add the symbol for *hand* at the bottom of *rain*. That makes *snow*. Rain and snow are both forms of water, but we can hold snow in our hands."

日 "Let's see what other characters we can combine to make new ones." Xiao Ming's mother walks to a fresh patch of snow. "Many words start with the character for *sun*."

"I know that character. It is a square with a line in the middle. I always imagine it's the sun winking at me," says Xiao Ming. The character for *sun* also means *day*.

"Draw three suns together—that's *sparkling*! Think of the sun reflecting off of a pond. The reflections look like little crystals sparkling on top of the water."

月 "*Moon* looks very much like *sun*, but the character has longer side strokes," his mother continues.

"It looks like a ladder reaching up to the moon," says Xiao Ming as he draws the character for moon with his finger.

明 Then Xiao Ming's mother draws a *sun* next to his *moon*. *"Bright,"* she says, "just like you. The character for your name." Xiao Ming smiles. The sun is setting and it is time to go home. He cannot wait for tomorrow to draw more pictures in the snow.

		Snow	xǔe
	雪		*(shre as in shred)*
	日	Sun	rī *(rur, pronounced with rounded lips)*
	晶	Sparkling	qīng *(ching)*
	月	Moon	yuè *(ureh as in red)*
	明	Bright	míng *(ming*)*

Pronunciation of words in parentheses are approximations of Mandarin Chinese.

* Xiao Ming's name is pronounced Schow Ming.

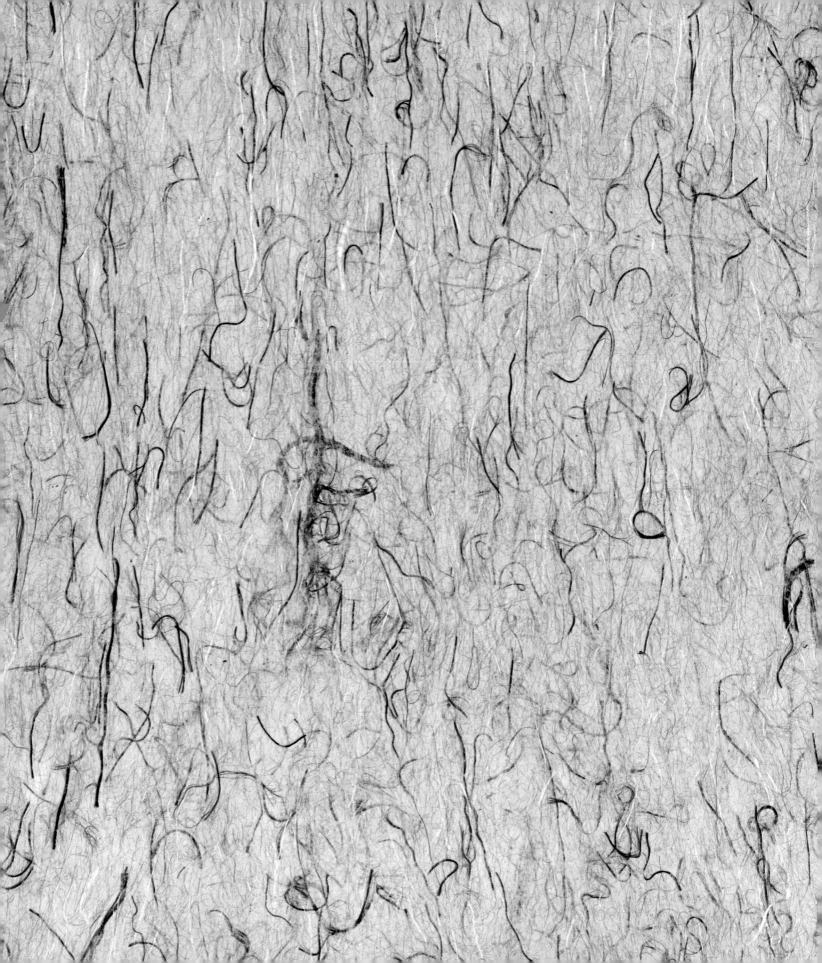

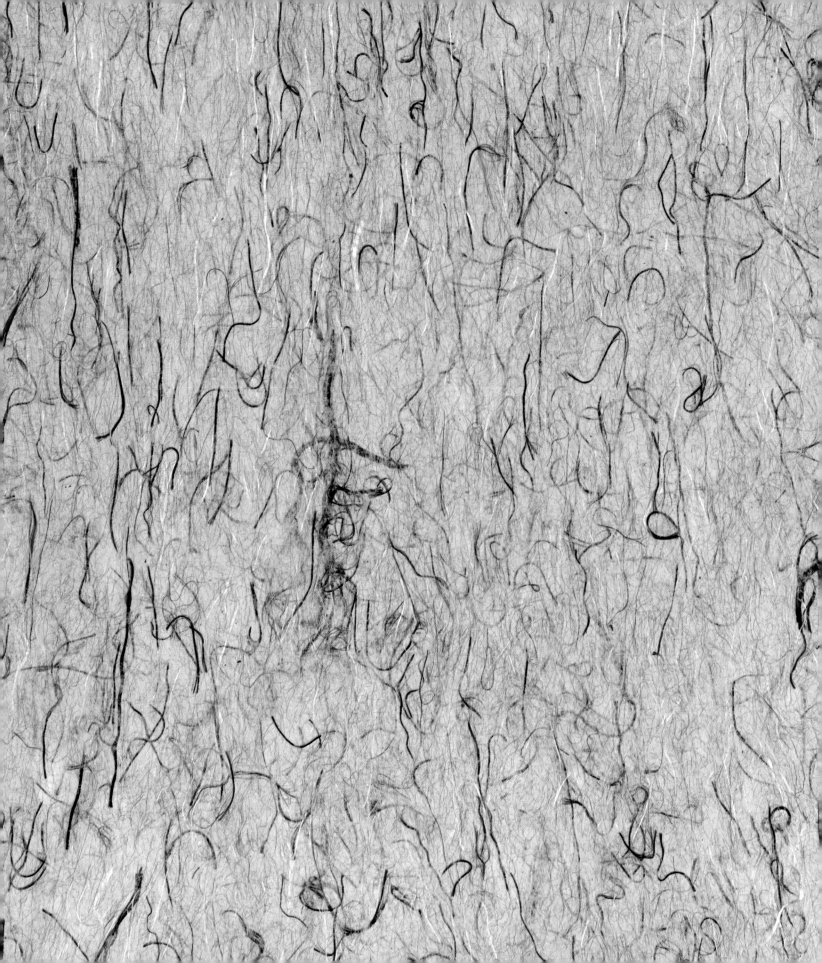